The AfterLife

of

Undead Ned

A Home Care

Survival Guide

The AfterLife of Undead Ned
A Home Care Survival Guide

Written by Valerie Doty
Illustrated by Abby Zechman

First Edition
Edited by Valerie Doty and Richard Goulde
Illustrated by Abby Zechman
English
Bound and Published by Lulu.com
United States of America

ISBN: 978-1-7336252-1-0

To my brother, Ned, who put his own life on hold for years to move back to his hometown and take care of his Mom, my stepmom, ensuring she would never realize her worst fears of having to move into a nursing home. It was a difficult and thankless job that he conducted with loving care.

Foreword

Welcome to the world of Undead Ned. His wife, Madge, will take you on a fun journey where you will learn the ins and outs of cleaning house the old-fashioned way, while preparing some good food, as Madge learns to navigate life with a literal *dead*beat husband.

You might identify with Madge and Ned. I was married for 12 years, and I know the struggle is real for some couples. When I first got married, I tried my best to be the perfect wife. I had a job, cooked all the meals, cleaned the house, and did all the laundry. My husband did nothing to help (at first). We argued a lot over little things like his dirty underwear all over the house and how little he contributed to the upkeep of our home. About four years into our marriage, I stopped picking up after him completely. A few days later, some new friends came over to the house, and there was my husband's dirty underwear on the living room floor. He was so embarrassed he scooped them up and never left clothes on the floor again.

About a week later, my husband asked when I was going to do laundry. I responded that I had just done it the night before. He indicated that he didn't have any clean underwear, and I replied that I had washed everything in the hamper. From that day on, his dirty clothes always made it to the hamper. No arguments and no doormat wife.

Of course, there's more to Madge's story than just charting a course into a happier and more equitable marriage. The right cleaning and food prep tips can pay dividends in lots of ways. While I'm not a cleaning expert, I grew up in a time when Moms didn't have jobs outside the home, and kids played outdoors without adult supervision. Keeping a tidy house was part of everyday living, and deep cleaning was a money saver. Our grandparents weathered the Great Depression and taught our parents the value of a dollar. It was important to clean and maintain everything in the house so it would last as long as possible. Proper care can double, maybe even triple, the life of everything you own. Replacing furniture, flooring, appliances, draperies, or any other big-ticket item every 5 or 6 years can seriously bite into your disposable or retirement income. My own drapes are over 30 years old because I followed the tips in this book. My stepdad made these drapes for me; he's gone now, and I will treasure them for as long as they last. Now I'm sharing all my accumulated experience with you.

I hope that Madge and Ned's story brings to life the wonderful partnership two people can have while building a home filled with love and respect. Cleaning house is one part of that journey that affects all the health aspects of the family—financial health, physical health, and mental health.

But please note, brains and eyeballs were only added to the recipes as part of the story and should not be added to any of the recipes in real life!

Enjoy!

Valerie Doty

Part 1

Chapter 1

Once upon a time, there was a beautiful princess named Madge and her handsome prince, Ned. They had two small children and lived in a beautiful castle on top of a picture-perfect, aspen-covered mountain. Every day, the prince roamed his kingdom while the princess and all the servants cared for the children and the castle. It was a beautiful dream. It was Madge's dream...

Madge shook her head to disperse the dream clouds and get back to reality. She knew Ned loved her and the children, but he was no prince. He wasn't even much help around the house. It was hard for Madge to hold down a full-time job, raise the children, cook the meals, and clean the house all by herself.

Then came the virus, which infected poor Prince Ned. Madge's once perfect family was now struggling to find a new normalcy. Living with a zombie was like being a single parent with one more, very large child, who ate weird things and smelled very bad. Oddly enough, Madge was finding that her life hadn't changed very much.

Working from home while her kids were in school was a godsend. Not having to commute to work gave Madge more time to tend to her house and family. She needed all the time she could get. Madge was tired, a lot.

* * *

Before the virus, Prince Ned had been an ok husband. He worked hard at his job and loved Madge and their children very much. The whole family played at the park on the weekends and talked about vacationing at the beach. Then one day, all that changed. In the middle of cooking dinner, the TV blared the news: the world had been hit by a virus.

Details were few and sketchy, but there was a hint of an explosion somewhere in the U.S. and the President had declared DefCon 3. Like the flip of a switch, the world shut down. As she was cooking, Madge had no idea this would be the last 'normal' meal they would enjoy for some time.

The next morning, Madge hopped out of bed as usual. No Ned. Making her way through the house, she finally found Ned standing in a corner, facing the wall. His legs were moving, but Ned was going nowhere. It was clear there was something very wrong with Ned. Should she take him to the emergency room or call their regular doctor? Madge picked up the phone and called NoBrain-E-R. That's how she learned the bad news. Ned had contracted the virus.

Madge raced her family to the NoBrain-E-R. The diagnosis? Ned had joined the Undead. Fortunately, the rest of the family was unaffected by the virus. Madge cried as the attendant fitted Ned with his DeathWatch. Ned had become a BombZomb. Something they didn't know— something the movies and books never revealed—zombies had an expiration date. One day, the BombZombs would self-destruct into a puddle and never walk the Earth again.

Madge knew the children would cry, too. Their Dad was now their BombPop. What would they do without their warm and loving dad? How would they mature with a BombZomb as a father figure?

Time for a little courage. Everyone was hungry, but no one felt like eating. Madge knew they could not bounce back on empty stomachs. Perhaps her family would not be able to resist a healthy dose of ooey gooey chocolate. Time to make the best chocolate cobbler Madge could muster. Everyone ate; there were no leftovers.

Courage by Chocolate Cobbler

1 – 7-ounce bag Chocolate Riesen Caramels, unwrapped
1 – 8x8x2-inch box devil's food cake mix
¼ – cup sugar
¼ – cup brown sugar
¼ – cup unsweetened cocoa powder
1⅓ – cups Kahlua or strong coffee
Vanilla ice cream, optional

Preheat the oven to 350°F. Lay the caramels on the bottom of a 9x9x2-inch pan. Prepare the cake mix according to package directions and drizzle the batter over the caramels. Don't worry about spreading the batter around the pan or into the corners.

In a medium saucepan, combine the sugar, brown sugar, cocoa, and Kahlua or coffee over medium heat, stirring regularly. As soon as the sugars are dissolved and the liquid is smooth, pour the Kahlua sauce over the cake batter. DO NOT STIR. Bake the cobbler for 45–50 minutes, until the cake looks firm.

Remove the cobbler from the oven and let it sit for 15 minutes. Sprinkle powdered sugar over the cobbler and serve it warm with vanilla ice cream. A person feels taller, and the world's problems always seem smaller, with chocolate.

Chapter 2

For someone who ate brains, Undead Ned didn't seem all that smart. Crooked and stinky, he wandered around the house aimlessly, grunting and dragging one leg. He hadn't showered or changed clothes since the virus. Madge didn't know what to do. After all, you can't kill someone who's already dead, no matter how offensive they've become.

Ned lost his job. Not only had he lost his ability to perform his daily duties, but the other employees were afraid of him; and storing brains in the company refrigerator was a bit disconcerting.

Declaring DefCon 3 didn't give any indication whether the President thought the virus was an act of war or more of a matter for Homeland Security, but it was clear the military was on high alert, and the government was funding a lot of research. The administration hadn't released any information from their experiments. Why were some people affected by the virus and others were not? No one seemed to know, but Madge was grateful not everyone in her family had been infected.

No one knew what the BombZombs could do, but they were quickly learning what the BombZombs couldn't do. Once infected, the BombZombs could no longer drive a car, raise their arms above their heads, or do anything that required brainpower. Madge would have to experiment with Undead Ned on her own. She sat down and, through the tears, made a plan.

Perhaps Undead Ned was trainable? There had to be something he could do on his own. Madge just couldn't take on a new babylike human as big as Undead Ned and continue to run the household as a single parent. It was just too much. Maybe it was time for Madge to declare DefCon 1 on her home.

The first order of business had to be making Ned less offensive. Besides, Madge didn't want her son to think it was ok to stop showering and smell bad. None of that 'like BombPop like son' stuff in this house. Tomorrow would kick off a new life for Madge and her family, beginning with a simple shower for Ned. Meanwhile, the kids would be home from school soon and Madge needed to start dinner. Madge learned early on to avoid beans and other flatulence producing foods. There ain't no fart like an Undead fart! A better option: winner, winner, chicken dinner.

Birdbrains

1 – tablespoon butter or margarine
1½ – pounds boneless skinless chicken pieces
1 – 10-ounce bag frozen spinach, optional
1 – 6-ounce box chicken flavored stuffing mix
½ – cup milk or cream
1 – 10.75-ounce can condensed cream of chicken soup
1½ – cups shredded cheddar cheese
10,000 – chicken brains, optional[1]

Remove any excess fat from the chicken. Melt the butter in a large skillet over medium high heat. Brown the chicken on both sides. Meanwhile, prepare the stuffing according to the package directions, except put the frozen spinach in the water before bringing to a boil. After fluffing the stuffing, stir in the chicken brains and spread the brain stuffing over the chicken in the skillet, on medium heat.

In a small mixing bowl, blend the soup and milk and pour the soup over the chicken and stuffing. Sprinkle the cheese over the chicken and cover the skillet. When the soup starts to bubble, reduce the heat to low. Simmer the chicken for 20 minutes, until the chicken is fully cooked.

This dish satisfies the BombZomb's cravings while masking the brain flavor for the rest of the family.

---

[1] *Chicken brains are only for zombies and should not be added in real life!*

Brain Power Salad

Dressing:
¼ – cup red wine vinegar
¼ – teaspoon ground mustard
2 – tablespoons honey
2 – tablespoons vegetable oil

Vegetables:
1 – 12-ounce bag romaine lettuce
1 – 8-ounce package sliced fresh mushrooms
2 – plum tomatoes, sliced
¼ – cup chopped walnuts
Brain bits, optional[2]

In a small bowl, combine the vinegar, mustard, honey, and oil. Let the dressing sit until dinner so the flavors blend well. Pour the lettuce into a salad bowl. Top the lettuce with the mushrooms, tomatoes, and walnuts. Toss the salad with the dressing just before serving. *Garnish with brain bits.* Madge hoped the brain foods in this salad would slow Ned's DeathWatch.

Brain Cloud

2 – cups water
1 – 6-ounce box strawberry Jell-O
1 – 10+ ounce prepared angel food cake
2 – 10-ounce bags frozen strawberries
1 – 8-ounce tub Cool Whip, thawed

In a large saucepan over high heat, bring the water to a boil. Meanwhile, tear the angel food cake into small pieces and distribute the pieces evenly in a 13x9x2 serving dish. As soon as the water starts to boil, remove the pan from the heat and stir in the strawberry Jell-O until the Jell-O is dissolved. Add the frozen strawberries to the Jell-O and stir until the Jell-O starts to thicken. Immediately stir in the Cool Whip and pour the mixture evenly over the angel food cake. *Sprinkle braindrops on the cloud.* Refrigerate the cloud for at least 2 hours before serving.

---

[2] *Brains are only for zombies and should not be added in real life!*

Chapter 3

The next morning, Madge pointed Ned at the clock. It was straight up 7:00am. She pulled off his clothes and shoved him into the shower. Madge showed Ned how to wash and then dressed him in clean clothes. Madge had purchased the strongest aftershave she could find and sprayed it liberally over Ned. Covering up Undead smell requires serious scent augmentation. Later, she would have to add Velcro® to all the right seams in his clothes so he could re-learn to dress himself.

Madge repeated this process every day at 7:00am until Ned started showering without her direction. Once in a while he would forget to take off his clothes, but the undeniable takeaway from the daily showers was that Ned was trainable. Using the clock to activate the process was brilliant. The Undead don't sleep and have no concept of time, so a trigger is needed to create a routine. The only question, should Madge buy a 24-hour clock or just let Ned perform his routine twice a day? A 24-hour clock would give Madge more control, but the way Undead Ned smelled warranted two showers a day.

Having proven Ned was trainable, Madge needed to find out what else he could do. She just couldn't go on working full-time and taking care of the house, the kids, and Undead Ned. Madge needed help. Madge called the NoBrainsCan hotline to let them know the BombZombs were trainable and asked for advice on what to do next. They were no help. What good was a hotline if they wouldn't share what NoBrains could do? Madge needed time to think, so she started making dinner. While BombZombs crave brains and must have them every day, the Undead body still needed a balanced diet to keep going and maybe slow down the DeathWatch. Madge had learned to disguise the hated vegetables so Undead Ned would eat them willingly. Tonight's dinner: a juicy meatloaf casserole. Easy to make and plenty of time to think.

Meathead Loaf

1 – small onion, chopped
1 – teaspoon red pepper flakes, optional
½ – cup breadcrumbs or wheat germ
1 – teaspoon garlic powder
3 – eggs
1 – teaspoon salt
½ – teaspoon black pepper
1 – 10-ounce bag frozen shredded spinach
3 – pounds 80% lean ground beef
1 – cup ketchup
2 – tablespoons brain powder, optional[3]

Preheat the oven to 350°F. Line a 13x9x2-inch pan with foil, shiny side down. Dump everything but the ketchup in a large bowl. Kneed the ground beef mixture until combined. Shape the meatloaf in the middle of the pan. Spread the ketchup over the meatloaf and bake for 60-90 minutes. Allow the meatloaf to cool for 5 minutes before cutting and serving. The Undead will devour this meatloaf without question, and it will keep them from scratching at your head in the middle of the night.

Lemon Brain Freeze

1 – 6-ounce can frozen lemonade concentrate, thawed
1 – 16-ounce carton lemon sorbet, softened
1 – 8-ounce tub Cool Whip, thawed
1 – 9-inch prepared shortbread crust

In a large mixing bowl with a mixer on low speed, beat the lemonade and sorbet. Fold in the Cool Whip. Put the batter in the freezer for 20 minutes so it will mound in the crust. Spoon the lemonade mixture into the shortbread crust and freeze the pie overnight. Remove the pie from the freezer about 5 minutes before cutting. *Garnish with brain sprinkles.*

---

[3] *Brains are only for zombies and should not be added in real life!*

Chapter 4

Madge jumped out of bed feeling better now that she had a plan. Undead Ned was already in the shower. The training was working. Did Madge see a little color in Ned's cheeks? She wasn't sure. Maybe it was just the hot shower. BombZombs felt no pain, so there was no need to teach Ned to mix hot and cold water. And hopefully the super-hot water would kill any germs trying to grow in his Undead folds of skin.

With the showers and copious amounts of aftershave, Undead Ned was far more acceptable to be around, but he wasn't much fun. For the first time in her life, Madge could honestly say she was with someone who loved her for her brains.

As Madge dressed, she noticed the walls looked a little fuzzy with dust; but work called, and she didn't have time for cleaning right now. Living with a BombZomb was difficult enough without dealing with chunks of Undead Ned stuck to the walls. A light bulb flashed in Madge's head. Ned was prone to wandering the house while she worked, so why not use that habit to her advantage?

Using a feather duster was the first step of house cleaning. The duster scatters dust, hair, and pet dander to surfaces cleaned by other household chores like vacuuming, so Madge knew to always do the feather dusting first. A perfect job for Undead Ned to perform. After Ned finished showering, Madge attached feather dusters to both of his hands and helped Ned line up with a kitchen wall. Ned bobbed and weaved as he lurched forward; the Undead didn't have good equilibrium. Madge steadied Ned a bit and sat down for a minute. As Ned wandered, his feather duster hands brushed the walls. The twitches in his arms and hands acted almost like the rotating head of a toothbrush. Decaying Ned-shed trickled to the floor. Madge smiled a little, with relief. Ned could help around the house. He just earned his first Madge Badge in Madge's Good Housekeeping Training Program.

Madge quickly served breakfast so she could get the kids to school and put in her eight hours of work. Ned could eat while Madge was bussing the kids. Madge looked around as she walked out the door; the walls looked cleaner, but the floors looked dirtier where Ned had dusted. Madge frowned as she decided to deal with the floors later. Was Ned shedding a little less?

Scatterbrains

12 – large jalapeños
1 – 8-ounce package bacon, fried and crumbled
1 – dozen eggs, scrambled in bacon grease
4 – green onions, chopped
1 – cup shredded cheddar jack cheese
1 – 16-ounce block Colby-Jack cheese
1½ – teaspoons cilantro
1½ – teaspoons cumin
1 – teaspoon oregano
1 – slice brain sausage, optional[4]

Preheat the oven to 375°F. Line a 15x10-inch jellyroll pan with foil, shiny side down. Cut the jalapeños in half lengthwise and scoop out the seeds and ribs with a grapefruit spoon. Lay the peppers on the foil, open side up. In a small mixing bowl, combine the eggs, bacon, green onions, shredded cheese, cilantro, cumin, and oregano. Spoon the mixture into each pepper half. Chop the brain sausage and scatter it over the egg mixture on the BombZomb's peppers. Slice the block of cheese into 24 thin slices and lay a slice on top of each stuffed pepper. Bake the peppers for 20–30 minutes, until the cheese is starting to brown. Cool for 5 minutes before serving. This dish is sure to satisfy the Undead's morning grumblies.

---

[4] *Brain sausage is only for zombies and should not be added in real life!*

Braindead Lemon Salad

1 – cup water
1 – 3-ounce box lemon Jell-O
1 – heaping cup miniature marshmallows
1 – 8-ounce bar cream cheese, softened
1 – 8-ounce tub Cool Whip, thawed
½ – cup mayonnaise
1 – 20-ounce can crushed pineapple, do not drain
1 – 3-ounce box cherry Jell-O
Whipped brain sweets, optional[5]

In a small saucepan over high heat, bring the water to a boil. Remove the pan from the heat and stir in the lemon Jell-O, until the Jell-O is dissolved. Add the marshmallows and allow the Jell-O to cool to room temperature, stirring occasionally.

In a large mixing bowl with a mixer on medium speed, combine the cream cheese, Cool Whip, and mayonnaise. Reduce the mixer speed to low and pour in the lemon Jell-O. Stir in the pineapple by hand. Pour the Jell-O mixture into a 3-quart shallow dish and refrigerate until set.

Make the cherry Jell-O according to the package directions and gently pour the warm cherry Jell-O over the chilled lemon Jell-O. Refrigerate until set. Garnish with brain sweets.

---

[5] *Whipped brains are only for zombies and should not be added in real life!*

Chapter 5

Madge was revolted by the lumps of rotting Undead flesh on the floor. She didn't want the children to be scarred for life, dreaming of undead chunks coming to life and crawling on the bed in the dark of night, rubbing against their innocent little heads! No one wanted that nightmare.

Now that Undead Ned had mastered feather dusting, Madge was able to downgrade to Household DefCon 2 and see if Ned could be taught to vacuum. Thankfully, Madge had purchased a powerful vacuum, although she'd had no idea what weird chunks would be awaiting that vacuum when she bought it. Time to see exactly what this fancy vacuum could do; would the vacuum choke on the Undead blobs or breeze its way across the carpet?

First, Madge tried taping the vacuum handle to Ned's hand, like what she had done with the feather dusters, but the push-pull action just wasn't in Ned's realm. Then it dawned on her: tie the handle to the back belt loop of Ned's jeans and send him off to wander.

Undead Ned was good at following the walls but needed some encouragement to vacuum the entire room. Madge tried fashioning part of a fishing pole with a dangling brain nugget on Ned's head, but his head was so shaky he just ended up in a corner. Then Madge decided to have the kids hide small chunks of brain around the room, much like the keepers at the zoo scatter fruits and vegetables for the gorillas to forage. Their BombPop could hunt down the tiniest tidbits of raw brain and drag the vacuum over the entire carpet. Madge heard hunks of dirt and flesh being sucked into the vacuum cleaner. Score! Madge just needed to make sure she checked the bag regularly to empty it.

Sometimes, the kids would move the brain niblets just before Ned got to them. Laughter rang throughout the house as they watched their BombPop begin to turn and sniff, desperate for that next brain treat. Madge let it go. It was a harmless prank considering Undead Ned didn't have the brain power to realize he was being tricked. Better it be a game than a nightmare. Madge finished her work and started dinner. BombPop had earned his second Madge Badge in Madge's Good Housekeeping Training Program.

Was there a glint in Ned's Undead eyes as he gobbled a morsel of brain? Surely not.

Brain Tubers

6 – large baking potatoes, cleaned
1 – tablespoon olive oil
1 – bulb garlic
½ – cup butter
1 – 8-ounce bag shredded cheddar cheese
chives and bacon bits, to taste
1 – cup chopped brains, optional[6]

Preheat the oven to 350°F. Cut each potato in half lengthwise and wrap the whole potato in foil, dull side out. Place all the foil–wrapped potatoes on the middle rack in the oven and set the timer for 30 minutes.

Cut the top off the garlic bulb so that the tip of each clove is cut off. Remove any dry layers of skin that are flaking off. Loosely, wrap the bulb in foil to form a cup around the bulb and drizzle the olive oil over the garlic. Seal the top of the foil. When the timer goes off, place the garlic in the oven with the potatoes. Set the timer for 45 minutes. When the timer goes off, remove the garlic and potatoes from the oven. Open the foil on all the potatoes, so they can cool a little before handling them.

In a small saucepan over low heat, melt the butter and squeeze the garlic paste out of the bulb and into the butter. Discard the remaining garlic skin. If there's a little garlic–flavored oil left in the foil, stir it in with the butter. Scoop the potato out of the skins and place the potato skins side-by-side in a 13x9x2-inch pan. Stir the butter and brush the inside of each potato skin with the garlic butter.

In a medium mixing bowl, combine the scooped potato with the remaining garlic butter. Mash the potato with half-and-half, buttermilk, or milk. Salt and pepper to taste. Fill the skins with the mashed potato. Sprinkle brains, shredded cheese, chives, and bacon bits over the potatoes and put the skins back in the oven just long enough to warm the mashed potato and melt the cheese, about 15–20 minutes.

---

[6] Brains are only for zombies and should not be added in real life!

Rack Your Brains

2 – pounds fresh green beans
1 – pound bacon
½ – cup butter
½ – cup brown sugar
1 – teaspoon garlic salt
1 – tablespoon soy sauce

Preheat the oven to 350°F. Use a pan just big enough to hold all the brainracks in one layer. Break off the stem on the end of each bean and discard the stems. If the beans are extra-long, cut them in half. Wrap 6–8 beans in a half strip of bacon and push a toothpick through the bacon to hold it in place. Lay each brainrack in the pan.

Melt the butter in a small saucepan over low heat. Remove the butter from the heat and stir in the brown sugar, garlic salt, and soy sauce. Pour the syrup over the brainracks. Bake the green beans for 30–45 minutes, until the bacon is done, and the syrup is thick and bubbly.

Brainless Fruit Salad

1 – 16-ounce tub sour cream
2 – tablespoons lemon juice
¾ – cup sugar
⅛ – teaspoon salt
1 – banana, sliced
1 – 8-ounce can crushed pineapple, drained
¾ – cup dark sweet cherries
¼ – cup chopped pecans, optional

In a large mixing bowl with a mixer on low speed, beat the sour cream, lemon juice, sugar, and salt until well blended. Stir in the remaining ingredients by hand. Pour the fruit salad into a small mold or paper cupcake liners and freeze. Take the fruit salad out of the freezer a few minutes before serving.

Chapter 6

Typically, Madge would clean house with vinegar and water before attacking the bathroom, but Madge knew she would never be able to train Ned about water-based cleaners versus oil-based cleaners and their distinct applications. Besides, he might 'clean' the paint and finish right off their furniture and woodwork. So, Madge decided to save all the dusting tasks for herself. And the toilet. Madge could never trust Undead Ned to clean the toilet. Who knows where that toilet water, and possible floaters, might end up. Take your wins where you can get them and do the rest yourself. Madge downgraded her house to DefCon 3. That felt so good!

Having Undead Ned shower increased his shedding. There was Ned-shed all over the shower stall. Madge checked the shower drain regularly, tossing the larger chunks of hair and flesh into the trash. There was only so much BrainoDraino could do. Madge wondered if Undead Ned might be able to clean the shower? Undead Ned could dust. Undead Ned could vacuum. It was a distinct possibility that Ned could clean the shower.

Madge decided to try fashioning shoes and gloves out of scrub brushes; after all, Ned couldn't walk straight anyway, so shoe-scrubs might just work out. When Ned wandered to the shower at 7:00, Madge squirted some tub-n-tile cleaner on the shower floor and walls, attached his scrub brush shoes when he stepped on them, gloved his hands, and waited while Ned lurched and slid all around the shower stall. Sure enough, the shower glowed when Ned exited.

Madge removed Ned's sloshie-galoshies and positioned his hands to scrub the sink. This was working. Madge was elated. Ned had never cleaned when he was alive. Maybe there was something to be said for being Undead. Maybe Madge had learned to stop worrying and love her BombZomb. She was sure she saw a glint in Ned's eye and that grunt sounded a lot like 'love you' as she removed his hand-scrubs. Then she proudly sewed the Level Three Madge Badge for Madge's Good Housekeeping Training Program onto Ned's shirt sleeve.

With Ned taking on some of the household responsibilities, Madge felt less rushed and stressed as she got the children off to school and sat down to work. Especially now that the kids were old enough to make their own breakfast, usually their favorite cereal. With a relaxed and open mind, Madge was able to wow her coworkers that day, and it encouraged her to see the bright side of keeping BombPop around. During a break, Madge started dinner.

Hairbrained Shrimp

½ – cup butter
2 – teaspoons freeze-dried minced garlic
½ – teaspoon fennel seed
1 – good-sized pinch saffron
½ – teaspoon dried parsley
½ – teaspoon chives
2 – tablespoons olive oil
1 – pound large shrimp, peeled and deveined
5,000,000 – shrimp brains, optional[7]

Melt the butter in a large skillet over medium heat. Stir in all the seasonings, brains, and oil. Salt and pepper to taste. Add the shrimp and sauté until the shrimp is done, stirring often. Serve with angel hair pasta. It's very entertaining to watch a BombZomb try to eat angel hair pasta!

Mind Blowing Peanut Butter Crownies

1 – 13x9x2-inch box brownie mix
24 – .55-ounce standard size Reese's Peanut Butter Cups
1 – 16-ounce roll refrigerated Reese's peanut butter cookie dough
1 – can evaporated milk (optional)

Preheat the oven to 325°F. Line a regular-size 12–cup muffin tin with paper cupcake liners. In a medium mixing bowl, make the brownie batter according to package directions, substituting evaporated milk for the water for a thicker, richer brownie.

Slice the cookie dough into 24 slices. Sugar cookie dough can be substituted for peanut butter cookie dough. Place a slice of cookie dough on the bottom of each cupcake liner. Press a Reese's Peanut Butter cup upside down on the cookie slice. Scoop a dollop of brownie batter onto the peanut butter cup. The brownie cups should look about ¾ full. Bake the crownies for 25–35 minutes, until the brownie outside looks done or some cookie dough has come to the top and turned brown. Remove the crownies from the oven and let them cool for 10 minutes before removing from the pan. Bake the remaining 12.

---

[7] *Brains are only for zombies and should not be added in real life!*

Chapter 7

Watching a BombZomb eat was particularly disgusting. Madge had tried taping a fork to Ned's hand, but he just kept stabbing himself in the face, confusing Ned and grossing out the children. So, Madge acquiesced to allowing BombPop to eat with his hands, cautioning the children not to copy this behavior. Sometimes, Ned would send food flying everywhere and what the dogs wouldn't eat stuck to the floor. Brains added a gooeyness to food that must be seen to be believed.

After successfully teaching Ned to shower, dust, and vacuum, Madge thought maybe she could teach him to mop. She knew it's best to vacuum up the big chunks on the tile first and then mop. So, after Ned had wandered the entire house with the vacuum cleaner, Madge put clean, wet pads on two mops and tied a mop to each of Ned's lower arms. Then she cranked up "Thriller" and turned Ned loose to dance through the kitchen. Madge couldn't remember when she first noticed BombPop dancing, but it was time to put it to use. It was quite a sight, watching Undead Ned do the BombPop Mop Hop, wobbling and floundering about the kitchen much like you would think Lurch would mop on *The Addams Family*. But the floor was getting clean while Madge was getting her work done. A win for everyone. Madge happily downgraded her home to DefCon 4 and awarded Ned the Level Four Madge Badge for Madge's Good Housekeeping Training Program.

This was Madge's typical day; day after day after Undead day. And each night, Madge dreamt of the princess in the castle. The life she wanted but would never have. How could have anyone dropped that bomb and released this virus? Could our own government have released the virus? The President wasn't telling. Was the damage permanent? Madge had been noticing little things that might indicate the virus was wearing off or somehow being cured. Undead Ned's DeathWatch had slowed, and he seemed to be changing back. Or was Madge just imagining what she longed for? The sparkle in Undead Ned's eyes, the glow in his cheeks, less shedding, murmurs instead of grunts, dancing.

No time to analyze now; Madge had work to do. The kids would be home soon. This was a good night for them to fix dinner. Madge was a little apprehensive about turning the kids loose in the kitchen, but they did not disappoint.

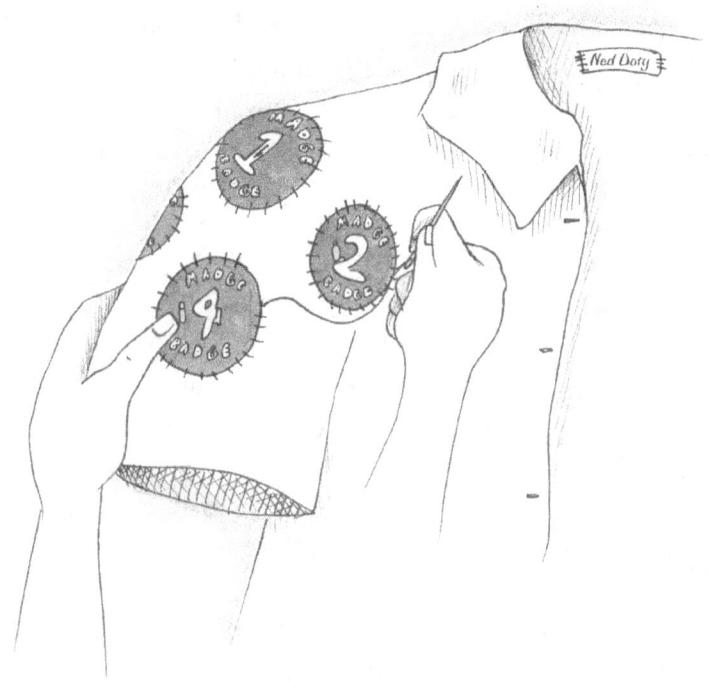

Cold Chain Slaw

½ – cup buttermilk
1 – cup mayonnaise
⅔ – cup sugar
1 – 16-ounce bag shredded cabbage
12 – eyeballs with roots and brain matter attached, optional[8]

In a large bowl, combine the buttermilk, mayonnaise, chopped eyeballs, and sugar. Add the shredded cabbage to the dressing and stir. Put the last 2 eyeballs on top of the coleslaw for decoration. Store the coleslaw in the refrigerator.

Wait at least 2 hours before serving so the sugar will dissolve into the dressing and lose its graininess. Eye see you gobbling up those veggies.

Viral Spirals

16 – slices soft white bread
1 – 8-ounce tub whipped cream cheese with chives or pineapple
1 – 12-ounce package thinly sliced bacon strips

Cut the crusts off the bread. Flatten each slice of bread with a rolling pin and spread a thin layer of cream cheese on the slices. Roll the slices into logs. Take a slice of bacon and spiral wrap the bread log. Put the rollups in the freezer until dinner time. It is best to separate the rollups with wax paper, or the bacon will freeze the logs together.

Preheat the oven to 375°F. Line a jellyroll pan with foil, shiny side down. Cut the frozen rollups into thirds. Place all the rollups on the foil and bake for 20–30 minutes, until the bacon is cooked through. *Sprinkle the BombZomb's spirals with a little brain powder*[9] *and serve.*

---

[8] *Eyeballs are only for zombies and should not be added in real life!*

[9] *Brain powder is only for zombies and should not be added in real life!*

Brain-free Raspberry Chocolate Chip Bars

¾ – cup butter or margarine, softened
1½ – cups quick cooking oats
1 – cup brown sugar
1½ – cups flour
½ – teaspoon salt
1 – teaspoon baking powder
1 – 18-ounce jar raspberry jam
1 – 6-ounce bag semisweet chocolate chips

Preheat the oven to 350°F. Put all the ingredients, except the jam and chocolate chips, in a large mixing bowl. With a mixer on low speed, beat the oat mixture until it's crumbly.

Press ⅔ of the oat mixture into a 13x9x2-inch pan. Stir the preserves to loosen them up and spread the preserves evenly across the crust. Sprinkle the chocolate chips over the jam and then the rest of the oat mixture over everything. Press the topping down lightly with the back of a spoon.

Bake the raspberry bars for 35 minutes, until they are brown and bubbly in the middle. Cool the raspberry bars to room temperature before cutting.

Chapter 8

On Pi Day (March 14), Madge knew her family would be happy eating pie all day. She used to love taking pies to work. She loved to see her coworkers smiling as they savored every bite of her homemade delicacies. And oh, how she loved the 'oohs', 'ahhs', and compliments. Sadly, there was none of that now that everyone worked from home. The world was changing hard and fast, but Madge clung to that ray of hope for better days with an open mind and a trusting heart.

Work was going well. Coworkers still laughed and joked in the team meetings. It was good to see friendly faces side-by-side on her monitor. Madge knew each of them was grateful for the distraction as they all dealt with their own BombZomb issues.

During the morning meeting, all Madge's coworkers asked what she was making on this special Pi Day. They all wanted to virtually savor the memories of pies gone by. Quiche for breakfast. A warm, comforting Pot Pie for lunch would give everyone a serving of the major food groups. BombPop could sprinkle brain pepper on his portion. Although he seemed to be consuming less brains these days. And of course, America's favorite: Apple Pie. Maybe some Peppermint Pie and Lemon Meringue Pie for snacking.

Madge remembered back in the 1970s, when Quiche became world renowned. No one in her circle spoke French. French Fries and French Toast were the closest they had ever come to France. So, they thought it was pronounced Quickie Loraine. Which made everyone twitter with laughter. Even now, Madge's coworkers laughed as she told the story. How

Madge yearned for those silly days that seemed so far away since the virus and its aftermath had blanketed the world.

Life seemed lighter now that Undead Ned was carrying some of the responsibility. He was showering/scrubbing the tile, dusting, vacuuming, and mopping all by himself. And he seemed to smell better. Ned's DeathWatch didn't seem to be moving much. Was that some stubble on Ned's rounded chin? Madge giggled and downgraded her home to the lowest level, DefCon 5.

Stroker Croaker Pot Pie

1 – 13.8-ounce tube pizza dough
2 – 12.5-ounce cans chicken breast
1 – 10.75-ounce can condensed cream of chicken soup
1 – tablespoon dried onion
¼ – teaspoon parsley
¼ – teaspoon thyme
¼ – teaspoon basil
1 – clove garlic
1 – 12-ounce bag frozen peas and carrots, thawed
1 – 8-ounce carton sliced mushrooms
100,000 – toad brains, optional[10]

Preheat the oven to 300°F. Grease a 9x9-inch Pyrex dish. In a large mixing bowl, stir together the chicken and soup, including the juice from the chicken. Add the onion and seasonings. Stir in the vegetables. Stretch the pizza dough to line the pan, with some overhang at each end. Spread the chicken mixture over the pizza crust. Sprinkle the toad brains over all or half of the pot pie. Stretch the overhanging crust over the top of the chicken mixture. Do not seal the crust, so the pie can breathe.

Optional: spread some butter on the top crust and sprinkle a little garlic powder and rosemary on top. Bake for 60-70 minutes, until the crust is golden brown, and the soup is bubbly. Serve hot.

----

[10] *Toad brains are only for zombies and should not be added in real life!*

Lemon Meringue Pie

Filling:
1 – 9-inch deep-dish frozen pie
  crust, thawed
1½ – cups sugar
3 – tablespoons flour
3 – tablespoons cornstarch
1 – dash salt
1½ – cups hot water
3 – egg yolks, slightly beaten
2 – tablespoons butter
½ – teaspoon grated lemon peel
⅓ – cup lemon juice

Meringue:
3 – egg whites
½ – teaspoon vanilla
¼ – teaspoon cream of tartar
6 – tablespoons sugar

Prepare the pie crust according to the package directions for a 1-crust pie. Cool the crust and change the oven temperature to 350°F. In a medium saucepan, combine the sugar, flour, cornstarch, and salt with a whisk. Slowly, whisk in the hot water. Bring the sugar water to a boil over medium high heat, whisking constantly. Reduce the heat to medium and cook two more minutes, still stirring. Remove the filling from the heat and put a little bit of the filling in a small bowl with the egg yolks. Stir and pour all of the egg mixture into the saucepan. Bring the filling back to a boil, stirring constantly. Cook the filling for two more minutes and remove from the heat. Stir the butter and lemon peel into the filling. As soon as the butter is melted, add the lemon juice slowly, mixing well. Pour the filling into the pie crust.

Make the meringue immediately, so the filling doesn't have time to cool and form a skin on top. Put the egg whites, vanilla, and cream of tartar in a large mixing bowl and beat them on high until soft peaks form. Add the sugar two tablespoons at a time and beat well after each addition. Continue to beat the meringue until the sugar is dissolved and stiff peaks form. Spread the meringue gently over the filling and seal the meringue to the edge of the pie crust all the way around, to prevent weeping. Use the back of the spoon to make spikes in the meringue. Bake the pie for 12-15 minutes, until the meringue starts to turn brown. Cool the pie and refrigerate it until the filling is firm. Cut the pie with a knife dipped in water.

Quiche Lorbraine

1 – frozen deep-dish pie crust
1 – pound bacon
3 – green onions
1 – 8-ounce bag shredded Swiss cheese
6 – eggs
1 – cup half-n-half
1 – dash crushed red pepper flakes
Brain juice to taste[11]

Bake the pie crust according to package directions for a 1-crust pie and allow it to cool a little. Set the oven temperature to 350°F. Meanwhile, cut the bacon into 1-inch pieces and fry the bacon to the crispness you prefer. Wrap the bacon in a paper towel to soak off most of the grease and crumble the bacon in the prepared crust. Chop the green onions, including the chive, and sprinkle over the bacon. Sprinkle a little more than half of the cheese on top of the bacon and onion.

In a small mixing bowl, whisk the eggs with the half-and-half and red pepper. Pour the egg mixture into the pie crust, allowing it to seep down between the bacon and cheese. Top the quiche with the rest of the cheese and bake the quiche for 40–45 minutes, until a knife inserted one inch from the edge comes out clean. Allow the quiche to cool for 10 minutes before cutting and serving. *Sprinkle a little brain juice over the BombZomb's piece and allow it to soak in before serving.*

---

[11] *Brain juice is only for zombies and should not be added in real life!*

Apple Pie

Filling:
1 – 9-inch deep-dish frozen pie crust, thawed
4 – Braeburn or Jonathan apples, peeled and cored
1 – tablespoon sugar
½ – teaspoon cinnamon

Shell:
¾ – cup margarine or butter
1 – cup sugar
1 – egg, beaten
¼ – teaspoon salt
1 – cup flour

Preheat the oven to 350°F. Slice the apples into the pie crust until the pie tin is full. Do not pack the apples; they will cook down. Also, don't pile the apples too high, or the shell will trickle off the pie before it cooks. Sprinkle the sugar and cinnamon evenly over the apples.

In a small saucepan, melt the margarine. Remove the pan from the heat and stir in the sugar, egg, salt, and flour. Spoon the thick batter over the apples to seep into the gaps and make a shell over the apples. Bake the pie for 45 minutes, until the top is completely light brown and done in the center. Serve the pie warm with ice cream.

Peppermint Pie

Chocolate Filling:
1 – 9-inch prepared chocolate cookie pie crust
1¼ – cups half-and-half
1 – 3.4-ounce box chocolate pudding mix
1 – cup semisweet chocolate mini-morsels

Peppermint Filling:
½ – 8-ounce bar cream cheese, softened
1 – 8-ounce tub Cool Whip, divided and thawed
½ – cup powdered sugar
½ – teaspoon peppermint extract, divided
6 – drops green food coloring, divided

Put the cream cheese in a large mixing bowl to soften. While the Cool Whip is still frozen, cut the topping in half and put half in the bowl with the cream cheese. Put the remaining Cool Whip in the fridge to thaw.

In a medium saucepan over medium high heat, cook the chocolate pudding and half-and-half almost to a boil, stirring constantly. When the pudding is thick, remove the pan from the heat and stir in the mini morsels.

With a mixer on medium speed, beat the cream cheese, half of the Cool Whip, and powdered sugar until fluffy. Add ¼ teaspoon of the peppermint extract and 3 drops of food coloring and beat until the cream cheese is a nice green color. Spread the cream cheese mixture evenly across the bottom of the pie crust.

Stir the chocolate pudding and spoon it into the pie crust. Carefully, spread the chocolate pudding evenly across the cream cheese layer. Refrigerate the pie for two hours.

Combine the remaining Cool Whip with 3 drops of food coloring and ¼ teaspoon peppermint extract. Spread the Cool Whip evenly over the top of the pie. Garnish with a few chocolate chips or cut up Andes mints. *Sprinkle with a few brain nuggets for Undead Ned, to help with that horrible Undead breath.*

Chapter 9

Madge crawled out of bed. Ned was already up. He turned to Madge and said, 'Good Morning.' Madge was so shocked all she could do was gurgle a little. Ned had already made breakfast and wiped down the counters. Ned was a totally different man after completing Madge's Good Housekeeping Training Program and earning his Level Five Madge Badge. BombPop was back to Dad, but better.

When the children came running down to the kitchen, Ned and Madge greeted them with smiles and hugs. The kitchen table was the cornerstone of all family engagement, as everyone talked and laughed about the day ahead. This would be the perfect time to teach the kids how to make Irish soda bread in honor of Saint Patrick's Day, as everyone decided what they wanted for dinner that night. It was best to wean Ned off brains slowly so his system could get used to the new diet. The whole family was excited to rid the house of all the brain-based products. And Ned could work on getting a job!

Ned's DeathWatch had fallen off. Was the virus gone completely? There was nothing on the news, but Ned was alive! He even smelled good. No more trips to NoBrain-E-R. No more calls to the NoBrainsCan hotline. Madge didn't know if the government had found a cure. She didn't know if all the BombZombs were awakening. All Madge knew was that her family was whole. She wasn't a princess and Ned wasn't a prince, but Madge was living the dream, and Ned was working to keep that dream alive, every day.

SNAFEW: Situation Normal - All Fantasies End Well.

Smiling Irish Soda Bread

½ – cup butter, softened
¼ – cup sugar
4 – cups flour
1 – teaspoon sea salt
1 – teaspoon baking soda
1 – cup raisins
1 – egg
1¾ – cups buttermilk

Preheat the oven to 350°F. Generously grease a 9x5x3-inch loaf pan. In a large mixing bowl, combine the sugar, flour, salt, and soda. Cut in the butter with a knife. Stir in the raisins and break up any clumps. Make a well in the center and stir in the egg and buttermilk. Pour the batter into the loaf pan and bake the bread for 50–60 minutes, until a toothpick comes out clean. Allow the bread to cool for 10 minutes, run a knife around the edge, and remove the bread from the pan. Cool to room temperature.

Mac's Headcheese

1 – 16-ounce package elbow macaroni
1½ – cups milk
1 – 16-ounce bar Velveeta cheese, cut into chunks
¼ – cup butter
1 – 16-ounce bag shredded cheddar jack cheese
2 – eggs
1½ – cups small chunks of brain matter when needed, optional

Prepare the macaroni according to the package directions. Preheat the oven to 350°F. In a 4-quart Dutch oven over low heat, combine the milk, Velveeta, butter, and 1 cup of the shredded cheese. Stir the cheese sauce until the cheese is melted. Add the eggs, *brain matter chunks*, and noodles. Salt and pepper to taste.

Pour the macaroni and cheese sauce into a 3-quart Pyrex baking dish. Sprinkle the rest of the cheese evenly over the macaroni. Bake the mac and cheese for 25 minutes, until the top is brown and bubbly.

Pennies From Heaven

1 – 10.75-ounce can condensed tomato soup
½ – teaspoon salt
¾ – cup white vinegar
1 – teaspoon Worcestershire sauce
¾ – cup sugar
1 – teaspoon prepared mustard
½ – cup vegetable oil, optional
2 – 14.5-ounce cans carrots, drained
1 – small green bell pepper, sliced
1 – small onion, sliced

In a medium mixing bowl, combine all the ingredients and marinate overnight, stirring occasionally. Drain off the marinade to serve. Make a wish and toss down some pennies.

Cherry BombZomb

1¼ – cups butter, softened
3¼ – cups flour
½ – teaspoon salt
1 – cup sugar
2 – 3.4-ounce packages Jell-O instant Lemon pudding mix
3 – 14.5-ounce cans pitted red tart cherries, do not drain
1 – teaspoon lemon juice
½ – teaspoon almond extract
¼ – cup slivered almonds

Preheat the oven to 350°F. In a large mixing bowl, cut together the butter, flour, salt, and sugar until crumbs form. Press ⅔ of the mixture into a 13x9x2-inch pan to make a crust. In a medium mixing bowl, stir together the pudding mix, cherries, lemon juice, and extract, until the juice looks a little thick. Spread the filling over the crust. Sprinkle the remaining flour mixture over the filling and press the topping down lightly with the back of a spoon. Bake the Cherry BombZomb for 50-60 minutes, until it's brown and bubbly in the middle. Cool to room temperature before cutting.

Part 2

Chapter 10

Madge's Good Housekeeping Training Program Decoded

Back in the olden days, women had one job and one job only: to create the perfect family and home. As women entered the workplace, there was less time to spend on cleaning house, and many techniques were lost. It also became fashionable to buy new rather than extend the life of current furniture, appliances, clothes, and the house in general ("Reduce, Reuse, Recycle").

Madge worked hard to preserve those original cleaning techniques and keep her home in mint condition. That way, she could spend her disposable income on fun vacations or save for retirement, instead of replacing her carpet and furniture.

Spring is a time of renewal and a great time for that extra deep Spring Cleaning everyone talks about. All winter, the kids are traipsing in dirt and moisture from the snow and rain. Plus, the house gets stuffy after being all closed up for the cold months. In the Spring, the weather invites opening the windows and allows the wind to refresh the rugs and blankets as they hang outside on the clothesline.

Status: Dead
Feather Dusting

Is feather dusting really cleaning, or just stirring up dust so it moves to a different location? It is certainly handy for dusting the walls around the dog's bed or anyplace dust seems to gather vertically, which can make the walls look dull and fuzzy. It's also good for ceiling fans, wall-hangings, window blinds, and other hard-to-reach places. There are dusters that encourage the dust to cling to them, so that's a step up from the old-fashioned, run-of-the-mill feather duster. Regardless, whether the dust sticks to the duster or drifts to another location, make feather dusting the first step in cleaning the house.

Many cleaning services now use the feather duster in lieu of cleaning with vinegar water or oil, which poses the question: do you really want the duster that just wiped the dirt and grime from your walls and ceiling fans to wipe the counters and tables where you prepare and eat food? Feather dusting may not be the best solution for all surfaces but it's a good first step in a cleaning regimen.

Note: It's natural to adjust the window blinds down but slightly open to cut back on the intense sun in the summer. However, angling the blinds down actually aims the sun's rays directly into the house, while turning the blinds slightly up reflects the sun's heat and still allows a view to the outside. After dusting the blinds, remember to turn them slightly up.

Status: Undead Vacuuming

Vacuuming can stir up dust, so always vacuum before dusting the counters and tables. It's best to have two people to vacuum: one person to run the vacuum cleaner and one person to pick up toys and lift furniture. If there is a soft brush extension for the vacuum hose, slide the brush over vents, lampshades, and TV screens. The brush is also good for the vents on the cable box and other electronics.

Before vacuums had handheld extensions and didn't get all the way to the edge of the flooring, old toothbrushes were used to clear the hair and dirt from along the baseboards. With their great extension hoses and specialty brushes, vacuums can now clean all those hard-to-reach places.

Vacuum cleaners can overheat and stop working when the bag is full or the hose is blocked. To avoid overheating the vacuum, check the bag or receptacle frequently to see if it needs to be emptied. Specifically, check the bag when starting to vacuum and then periodically when moving from room to room. If the vacuum does overheat, change the bag or empty the receptacle, wait a little while for the motor to cool, and resume vacuuming.

Status: Better-Off-Dead

Dusting Stage 1 - Water Based Cleaning

Glass and Mirrors Cleaner

½ – cup white vinegar
1 – quart water
2 – clean lint-free rags

Glass and Mirrors, this is not magic. Using a small (3 or 4 quart) bucket, mix about ½ cup of white vinegar with approximately one quart of water. Put one lint-free rag in the vinegar water for washing and carry one lint-free rag for drying.

It's best to use the fresh vinegar-water on food preparation surfaces first, so start with wiping down all the kitchen tables and counters. No need to wipe dry.

Next, wipe down all the glass. Take the wet rag out of the vinegar water and wring it until it's almost dry. Wipe the mirrors with the wet rag, rinsing the rag often depending on how dusty or toothpaste-riddled the glass may be. Then dry the mirrors with the dry rag using only vertical or only horizontal motions. Only windows and mirrors need consistency in the drying motions to avoid weird and distracting streaking.

Repeat this action for all windows and mirrors, and then any other dusty, dirty surface that is not composed of finished wood, including the top of the refrigerator. Painted wood should also be cleaned with vinegar water. The vinegar water is cleaning the paint, not the actual wood. The oil in furniture polish can discolor the paint so vinegar water is preferable.

Save the bathroom for last. Wipe down the counters, towel bars, and finally the outside of the toilet and toilet seat. When finished, dump the bucket of dirty water in the backyard. Vinegar is environmentally friendly, and some bugs don't like it, so it can have pest control benefits, too.

Always do this step—cleaning with vinegar-water cleaner—before dusting the finished wood in case a little vinegar water splashes on the finished-wood furniture. Water can ruin the finish on the wood (just like sweaty drink glasses can leave rings on a wooden table or bookcase), so oiling it immediately after drying off the water will help save the beauty of finished wood.

Clean kitchen tables with vinegar water. They aren't usually made from real wood but rather a faux-woodgrain Formica-type product. Kitchen tables are made for the daily wear and tear of hot plates and sweaty glasses.

Status: Sicker-Than-a-Dog

Dusting Stage 2 – Oil-Based Cleaning

The beautiful, natural wood pieces in the home need to be oiled to thrive and survive. Always dust natural wood with an oil-based furniture polish, like Pledge, Endust, or Old English. Don't use anything that comes in a hard cake; whatever dries it into a cake will dry your furniture.

If there are sticky spots from a spill, clean with vinegar water, dry with a soft cloth, and oil immediately. Natural wood furniture will stay glistening and healthy for a long time with proper care. Never set a spray can on wood furniture. The metal bottom can have rust or corrosives that will harm the finish on your beautiful furniture.

In fact, always use coasters on wood furniture. Never, ever put a container of liquid of any kind on a piano, not even a glass of water. If it spills into the keys or strings, the piano may be irreparably damaged. Madge's piano bench still bears the imprint of a friend's butt, after that friend sat down to play the piano immediately after swimming in the pool. The only way to fix a water stain or ring is to strip the entire piece of furniture, stain the wood, and put a nice finish overall.

Annually, oil all beautiful woodgrain furniture with a coat of lemon oil. The dining table, buffet, hutch, dresser, armoire, nightstands, coffee table, entertainment center, bookcases, end tables, and all other natural wood furniture will last generations with a little tender loving oil care.

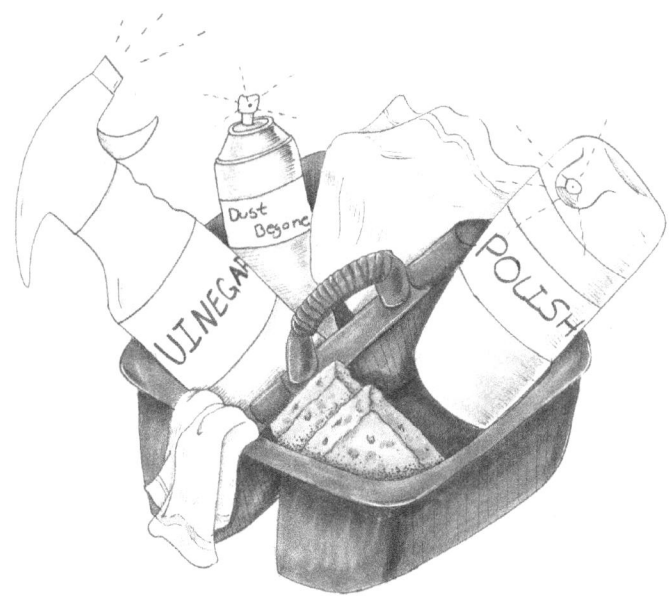

Status: Viral

Donning the Hazmat Suit and Cleaning the Bathroom

The toilet bowl can be cleaned with any commercial toilet product or white vinegar. Some toilet cleaners are toxic to dogs, so be sure to flush well after cleaning the toilet for all the dogs who like to drink out of the toilet. Continuous toilet bowl cleaning products are not usually good for dogs either.

The bathtub and shower walls can be cleaned with any commercial product or white vinegar or baking soda. Not only is a hand-held massage shower head good for those hard-to-reach places on your body, but it makes cleaning the tub and shower so much easier.

As you can see, white distilled vinegar is very handy. Bleach or a commercial anti-mold product can be sprayed on the bathroom tile to make mold disappear.

Important! Never, ever combine bleach and vinegar; together, those two chemicals create toxic chlorine gas. Similarly, never combine bleach and ammonia, which together also create a toxic gas. You can, however, mix vinegar with baking soda to make a volcano erupt in your bathtub.

Status: Alive-and-Well

Ancillary Cleaning

The Laundry:

There's no mystery to sorting laundry. Whites with absolutely NO color go in one pile and everything else in the other pile. Now these two piles can be divided into dress clothes (delicates) and everyday clothes or dark colors and light colors. Depending on your wardrobe, you may end up with four piles. Any colored clothing that is brand new, especially if it's red, should be washed separately at least once, or even twice, in case the color runs. The deeper the color, the more likely it needs to be washed more than once by itself. Read the instructions on the laundry products to see how to use them. Amway makes my favorite laundry products, as they contain less filler and are kind to sensitive skin.

There are two reasons to separate whites: (1) so they don't pick up color from the other clothes and (2) so you can bleach them. However, only use bleach when your natural whites are totally gross. Bleach gets out stains and brings back that glistening white you purchased, unless the clothes are made of more modern fabrics where the white is a dye. In that case, bleach removes the white dye and leaves the clothes looking a little dingy. For newer fabrics, it's better to use white vinegar to brighten the whites. Add ½ cup vinegar to the wash or put it in the fabric softener tray for the rinse.

Blood is an entirely different animal. Blood stains fabric because tap water bursts the red blood cells allowing the red to be absorbed into the cloth. Don't rinse or launder the blood. Instead, spray the blood with hydrogen peroxide or distilled water and dab the blood out with a paper towel. Then launder the clothing.

Detergent boosters are available for those yard-work-dirty clothes. Bleach and boosters go in the wash cycle. Fabric softeners are available for both the washing machine and dryer. Softeners that go in the rinse cycle of the washer are the most comprehensive, since some delicates shouldn't go in the dryer. Delicates can air-dry on a clothes line, clothes rack, or sweater dryer. Drying clothes on a hanger should be avoided because it leaves cute little stretch lumps on your shoulders.

There are debates over water temperature. Many detergents are designed to clean in cold water so why spend the money on electricity to heat the water? Some washing machines automatically mix hot water with the cold if the cold water is below a certain temperature in the winter. The dryer gets pretty hot, if you're worried about temperature. Read the clothing labels to make sure you dry using the proper settings. Heat can shrink and fade clothing. Clean the dryer filter often. Leave the detergent tray open between washings to allow the tray, hoses, and pipes to dry quickly, avoiding mold growth and bad smells.

The Drapes:

If your curtains are washable, launder them yourself, treating them as delicates. Dry-clean-only drapes do not need to be dry-cleaned often, but they do need to have the dust removed annually. Dust makes the drapes look dingy, and it can rot the fabric. Once a year, one window at a time, take down your drapes and put them in the dryer for an hour. Do not use any heat; just tumble them on air-only. Clean the dryer filter often as you put in each set of drapes. Don't pack the dryer too full, so all the dust gets sucked out. Take drapes to the dry cleaner every few years to get them deep cleaned and pressed. If the weights in the bottom cuffs of the drapes are lost, insert a quarter for each weight.

The Furnace Filter:

Replace the furnace filter according to the filter instructions; some are monthly, and some are quarterly. You may need to change your filter more often if you have a big family or multiple pets. To trap the dust better in the fiberglass filters, spray both sides of the filter with cooking spray right before sliding the new filter into the vent.

Static Electricity:

Static electricity can be shocking in the winter. Fill a spray bottle with equal parts water and liquid fabric softener. Shake the bottle to blend the liquids and spray all the carpet and rugs in the house. Spray whenever sparks start to fly.

Carpet:

Have the carpet professionally cleaned once a year. Sand and dirt can grind into the carpet fibers and tear them apart like a razor blade. Professional machines have much better suction than the average vacuum cleaner, so they get a much deeper clean.

Buy a steam cleaner to spot clean after the kids or pets make a mess. Choose a steam cleaner with a long horizontal roller brush, not the disk brushes. The rounding motion of disk brushes can unravel the carpet fibers. Carpet cleaning annually is often a carpet warranty requirement.

Empty Tissue Boxes:

Keep an empty facial tissue box in the bathroom trash can. These are perfect for the disposal of used bandages, feminine products, medicine bottles, Q-tips, sticky cough drop wrappers, hairballs from combs and shower floors, wet cotton balls, etc., to contain the mess and keep the trash can clean.

Battery Leakage:

Changing batteries is easy, until you open a tool to find battery acid corrosion. The new batteries won't make proper contact until the corrosion is removed from the terminals. Mix 1 tablespoon of baking soda with 1 cup of warm water and clean the terminals with a Q-tip dipped in the soda-water. For larger batteries with a lot of corrosion, sprinkle baking soda directly on the acid corrosion to neutralize the acid before scraping it off. Goggles help protect your eyes from flying shards of dried corrosives.

Tool Caddy:

A 2-compartment or 3-compartment handled-tote is very handy on cleaning day. Most totes can hold several spray cans or bottles, tub and tile cleaner, toilet bowl cleaner, several rags and lint-free towels, and a scrub brush. There are some very nice molded bottle totes for cleaning, but they never seem to fit the bottles you actually have. Not only does the tool caddy help you stay organized for cleaning, it gives you a place to put wet rags as you move from room to room. When you finish cleaning, the used rags go in the laundry and fresh clean rags go in the tote for next time.

Enhancing the Olfactory:

Bad smells can come from anywhere, not just the Undead. This is where baking soda, vinegar, and potpourri become your best friends. You've probably read about or experienced various health issues related to commercial air fresheners, but there are easy alternatives to make your home smell good.

Baking soda has long been used to refresh the refrigerator. In fact, Arm & Hammer now makes a package specifically for the fridge. You can also sprinkle baking soda over the carpet and vacuum it up for odors in the carpet and vacuum cleaner. Arm & Hammer has an entire webpage dedicated to carpet cleaning and deodorizing.

Home Interiors used to sell wonderful candles you could warm in a mini crockpot (some manufacturers make small crockpots specifically for potpourri) and make the whole house smell good. You take three 2-inch candles, remove the wicks, and put the candles in the crockpot. As the wax melts, the smell is released. Candles from the grocery stores don't have enough scent to permeate the room like those Home Interiors candles did.

The mini crockpot is a great solution because there's no open flame and no chance of something boiling dry on the stove. To change scents, put the room temperature mini crockpot in the freezer until the wax freezes, remove from freezer, turn upside-down, and the wax will fall out. If the wax seems stuck, tap the crockpot on a towel or something soft that won't crack the crockery.

If you can't find strong smelling candles, the mini crockpot can be used for many scents. Fill the mini crockpot halfway up with water. Plug it in and add vanilla extract, vinegar, cinnamon, potpourri, apple slices, or anything else that smells good to you. And just that little bit of heat from the crockpot adds a warm, cozy feeling to the scent.

Congratulations! You've earned the Madge Badge of Life.

Appendix: Home Cleaning & Maintenance Checklists

Daily/Ongoing Tasks

- ☐ **Washing machine**: Leave the machine lid open and the detergent/softener tray extended when not in use, allowing everything to dry quickly and deterring the growth of mold.
- ☐ **Dryer:** Clean the dryer vent often.
- ☐ **Garbage disposal**:
  - ☐ Always run cold water when using the garbage disposal, even when grinding ice.
  - ☐ If the splash guard gets slimy or moldy, clean with vinegar water.
  - ☐ Do not put anything stringy, like celery or banana peels, into the garbage disposal.
  - ☐ Never pour grease down the drain, especially on the garbage disposal side of the sink..

Weekly Tasks

- ☐ Feather dust.
- ☐ Vacuum.
- ☐ Dust with water-based cleaner like vinegar and water.
    - ▫ Clean kitchen counters and tables.
    - ▫ Wash and dry mirrors.
    - ▫ Wipe anything that is not natural wood: appliances, lighting fixtures, books, clocks, electronics, desks, and knick-knacks.
    - ▫ Clean the drip pans under the stove burners or clean and polish the glass cooktop.
    - ▫ Wipe the toilet seat and outside of toilet last.
- ☐ Clean toilet bowl with commercial cleaner and toilet brush.
- ☐ Clean bathtub and sinks with commercial cleaner and scrub brush, not the same brush used in the toilet.
- ☐ Dust finished-wood surfaces with oil-based cleaner, like Pledge.
- ☐ Wash bedding.
- ☐ Mow the lawn.
- ☐ Trim bushes and trees.

Monthly Tasks

- ☐ **Garbage Disposal**: Grind ice monthly.
- ☐ **Swimming Pool**: Maintain monthly.
- ☐ **Pest Control**: Set up monthly, especially in Southern states where insects and vermin run rampant.

Quarterly Tasks

- ☐ **Swimming Pool**: Clean the filter quarterly.
- ☐ **Gas Generator**: Run quarterly.

Semiannual Tasks

- ☐ **HVAC System**.
    - ☐ Have maintained semiannually.
    - ☐ Replace furnace filters according to the directions on the filter.

Annual Tasks

First, deep clean the house (AKA Spring Cleaning).

- ☐ Start by performing normal routine cleaning.
- ☐ Use lemon oil on finished wood, including pedestals and legs.
- ☐ Clean ceiling fans, walls, light switches, doors, molding, and baseboards.
- ☐ Wipe cabinets and appliances.
- ☐ Wash slipcovers.

- ☐ Vacuum vents and speakers.
- ☐ Dust blinds, light fixtures, lamps, and lampshades.

Then, handle annual maintenance tasks.

- ☐ Wash windows (inside and out) and windowsills.
- ☐ Clean curtains.
  - ☐ Wash machine-washable curtains.
  - ☐ Put dry-clean-only drapes and comforters in dryer on air-setting for 60 minutes.
- ☐ Shampoo carpet.
- ☐ Vacuum or steam clean upholstery.
- ☐ Clean oven
  - ☐ Clean/replace oven liner
- ☐ Clean inside of refrigerator.
- ☐ Wash shower curtains and bathmats.
- ☐ Flip mattresses and wash bedding.
  - ☐ Add waterbed conditioner, if applicable.
- ☐ Wash dog and cat bedding.
- ☐ Sweep garage floor.
- ☐ Wash garage door and patio furniture.

Next, tend the yard.

- ☐ **Tend the yard**:
  - ☐ **Spring**:
    - ▪ Turn on sprinklers.
    - ▪ Turn on water at the street.
    - ▪ Program sprinklers according to city ordinances.
    - ▪ Check sprinkler heads for leaks.

- **Fall**:
  - Turn off sprinklers.
  - Shut off water at the street.
  - Drain Sprinklers
  - Shut off programming.
  - Wrap and cover outdoor faucets.

Multiyear Tasks

- **Curtains and comforters**: Dry-clean drapes and comforters every 5 years.

About the Author

Valerie Doty was born and raised in the Quad City area, a region of five cities in northwestern Illinois and southeastern Iowa, where she acquired an affinity for, and expertise in preparing, Midwestern comfort food from the wonderful cooks in her family.

With a bachelor's degree in Math Theory, she initially joined the world of Information Technology as the industry was skyrocketing in the Dallas, TX area. During her career in that field, Valerie met many coworkers who didn't cook for themselves at all. That lack of kitchen activity inspired her first book and kickstarted Valerie's mission to encourage people to return to the kitchen, bond with family members through cooking, and learn and save all their family-favorite recipes.

Valerie spends most of her spare time writing, enjoying her horses, and volunteering. You can visit www.lulu.com to find her first 2 books, '*Caveman Chemistry, Bringing Science Back into Cooking*', and '*My First Holiday Cookbook*'.